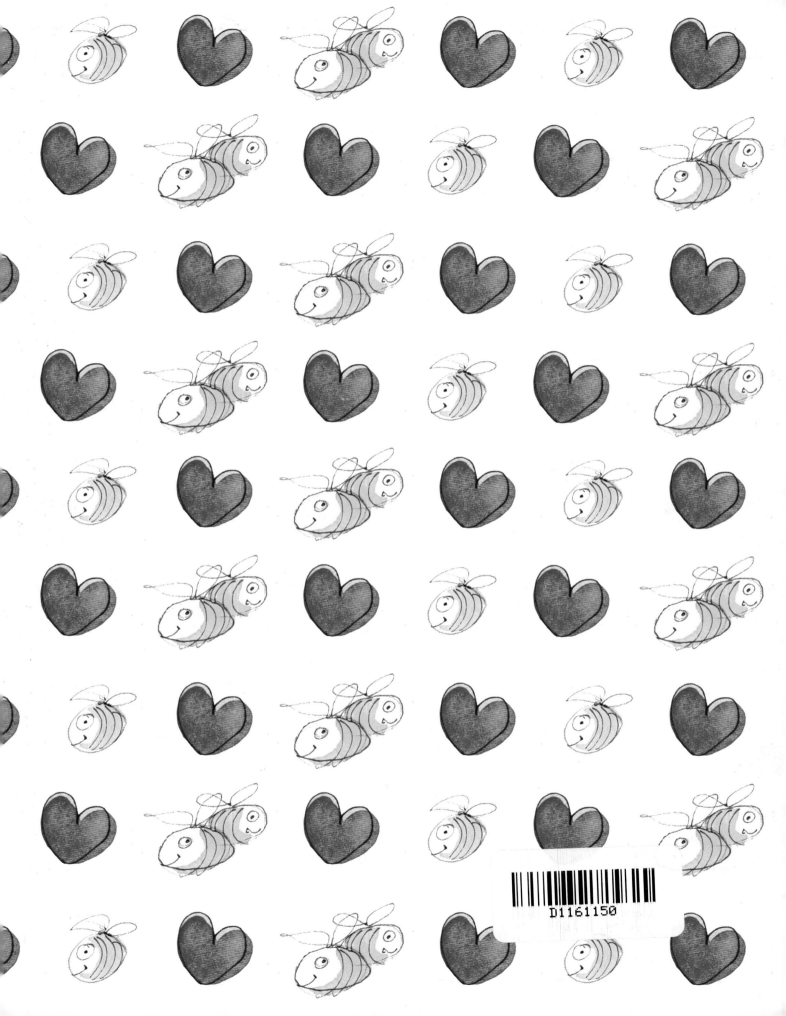

www.FlowerpotPress.com
DJS-0912-0196
ISBN: 978-1-4867-1887-0
Made in China/Fabriqué en Chine

Snuggle
When We Read This Book

Written by Joe Fitzpatrick
Illustrated by Marco Furlotti

I love when it is bedtime
and I know that you're nearby.
It makes my bedtime way more fun,
and here's the reason why...

I find you, and I hug you and say,
"Please come tuck me in!"

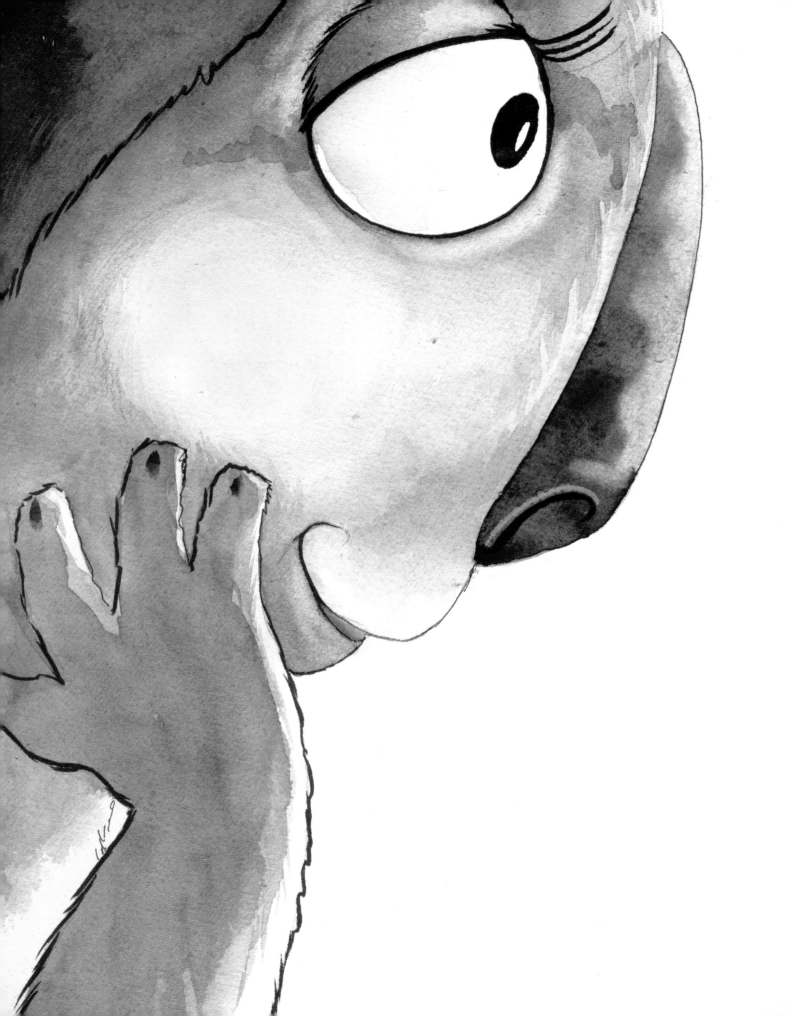

So we gather up my bedtime things,
and then we can begin.

We get this book, a cozy blanket,
and the pillows that we need.

And then I tell you one more thing
before we start to read.

I get in nice and close,
and then I whisper in your ear.

There's a rule for bedtime reading
that I think that you should hear.

We snuggle when we read at bedtime.
We love to read this way!

I try very hard to listen
and not doze off right away.

We snuggle when we read at bedtime.
Sometimes I rest my head.

Though at times I might close my eyes,
I've still heard what you said.

And when this snuggler falls asleep,
you let me sleep all night.

Yes, I love when it is bedtime
and I know that you're around,
because dozing off while snuggled up
helps me sleep safe and sound.

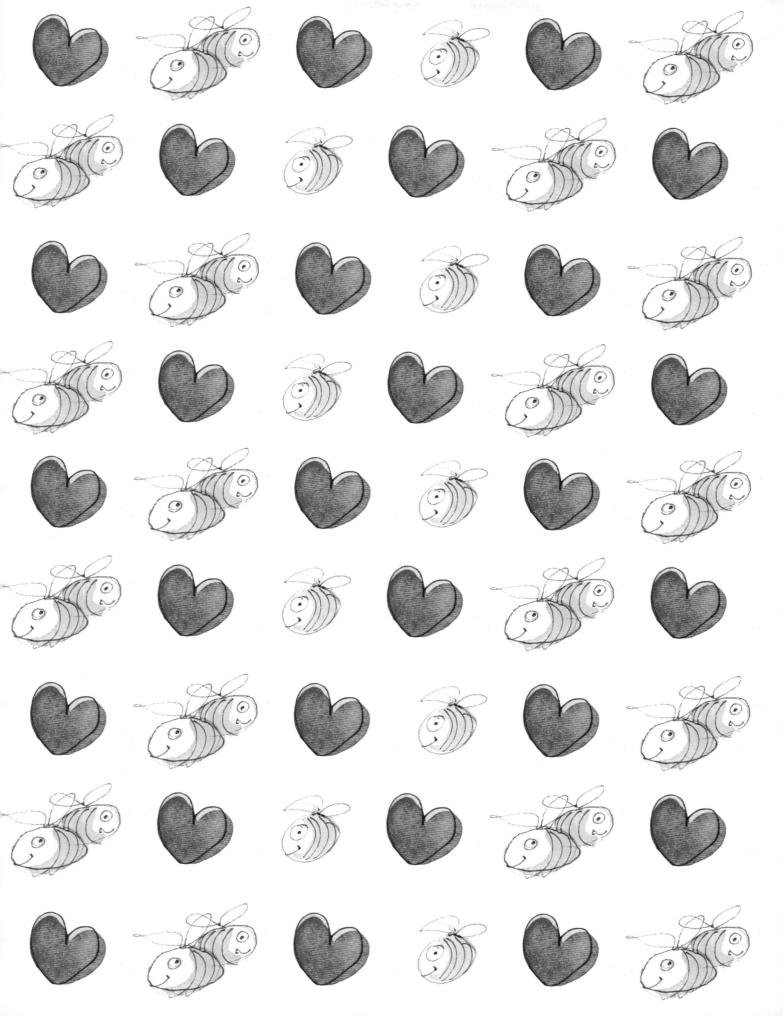

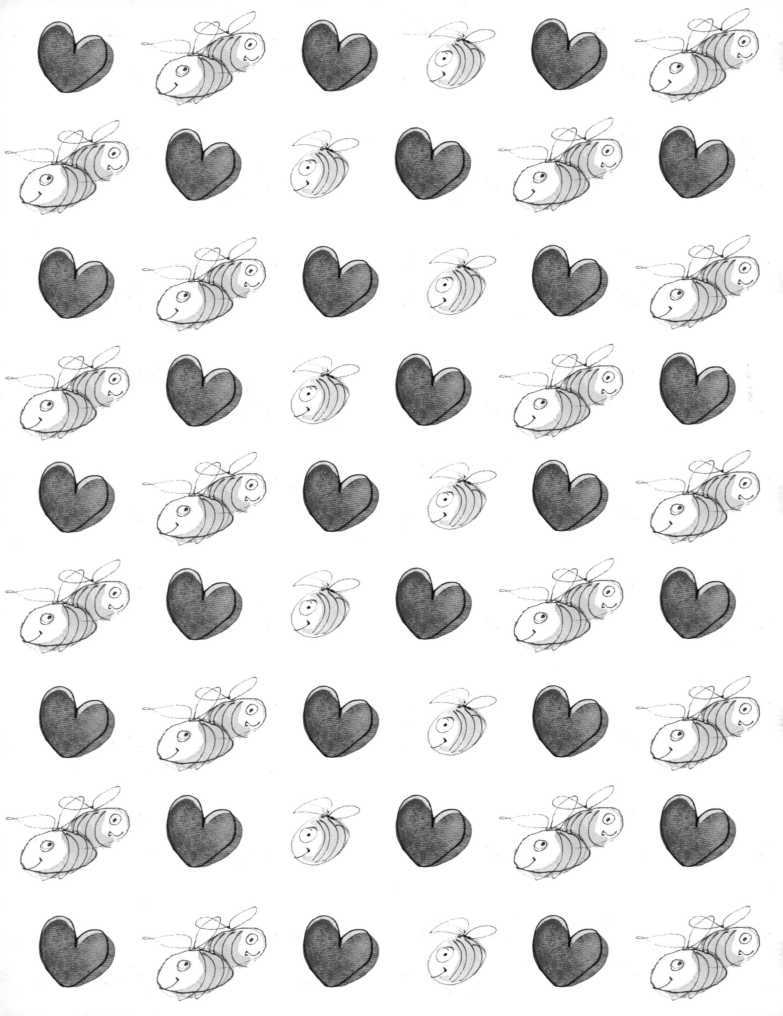